THE CASE OF THE CANCELLED CHRISTMAS

Disclaimer

Werewolves aren't real. They're just pretend, so you don't need to be scared or have nightmares. If you were to ask me if fairies are real? I'd say yes. Unicorns? Most definitely. And Father Christmas? I have his phone number.

But not werewolves.

I say this because the book that you are about to read has werewolves in it, just in case you didn't know.

If you don't want to read about werewolves, might I suggest you read another book? I'm sure you'll be able to find something to your liking at the local library or bookshop. Something about rainbows and kittens perhaps, or a nice old fashioned fairy tale?

However, if you do want to read about werewolves, it's time to turn the page...

P.S. Other things that aren't real include vampires, ghosts, zombies, evil witches, swamp monsters, Frankenstein's monster, closet monsters, basically any type of evil monster. They're all just make believe.

P.P.S. Unfortunately for me, clowns are real...

Chapter 1

It was three days before Christmas and the night of the full moon. Everywhere she looked, the world was covered in a blanket of soft white snow.

Jessica loved the snow. From making snowmen and having snowball fights, to running in her wolf form and diving into deep snowdrifts, everything about snow was wonderful.

"I'll go and hide again," William said, shaking the loose snow from his fur.

William had white fur in his werewolf form, and was the most difficult to spot when playing hide and seek in the snow. He had already hidden himself three times, but he didn't seem to mind being the one hiding and not seeking.

"One, two, three," Jessica counted with her eyes closed, working her way slowly towards one-hundred. The other wolves stood around her, their eyes closed as they counted along with her.

"Ninety-nine, one hundred!" Jessica said aloud as she opened her eyes. "Coming, ready or not!"

"I bet he's behind that hill again," Kiera said.

"No, he'll be behind that tree stump," Hannah suggested, raising her nose into the air and sniffing.

"Remember, Hannah," Oliver reminded her. "No werewolf senses, we have to look for him normally."

"That's not fair," Hannah protested. "William smells so bad it's impossible not to smell him." That made Kiera and Jessica laugh, and soon Hannah and Oliver were laughing along with them.

"This way," Jessica said at last, spotting William's tracks in the snow.

William had been careful to try to hide his tracks, taking big leaps and running around and around in circles, but Jessica hadn't been fooled. Amongst the disturbed snow, she had been able to spot a faint line heading through the clearing and towards the edge of the forest.

The other wolves ran along behind her, tails wagging and mouths hanging open as they enjoyed their game. It wasn't long before they arrived at the trees and began to look more carefully.

"We'll find you, William," Hannah called out.

"Not looking over there you won't!" William replied from somewhere to their right.

Jessica laughed and ran as fast as she could towards William's voice. "I've got you now," she said.

As Jessica ran around the thick trunk of a tree, she ran straight into William, both of them rolling over and over in the snow.

Chapter 2

"That was fun," William said. "Shall I go and hide again?"

"Maybe someone else should have a turn," Jessica suggested.

"I don't mind, really," William replied. "If I close my eyes, I'm almost invisible!"

That made Jessica chuckle, but a stern look from Oliver soon stopped her. "Oliver, what's the matter?" she asked.

"Can't you smell it?" Oliver replied. "There's something new in the forest, it smells strange."

Jessica raised her nose into the air and had a long, slow sniff. Oliver was right, there was a new smell in the forest that she hadn't smelt before.

"It smells a bit like deer," Jessica began. "I used to

chase them in the country, but they didn't smell exactly the same."

"I didn't think there were any deer in Swanholme Park," William said. "Squirrels and rabbits, maybe even a badger, but no deer."

"We've never smelled anything like it in all the times we've been here," Oliver agreed. "I think we should go and investigate."

Oliver took the lead as the other wolves followed slowly behind. There wasn't just one deer smell, Jessica noticed, there were lots of them. She counted nine different deer smells as they got closer.

Oliver crouched low as they neared the source of the smell, creeping forwards towards a gap in the hedge. As he pushed his snout through, he was met with a most unusual sight.

"They're not normal deer," Oliver exclaimed. "They're reindeer!"

#

Oliver was right, they were definitely reindeer. As the others poked their noses through the hedge, they were able to count nine reindeer, as well as a battered looking red sleigh half buried in the snow behind them. Most of the reindeer were lying down, licking wounds or sleeping, with only one appearing to stand guard.

"What should we do?" Jessica whispered.

"They look hurt," Kiera remarked. "We should go and see if we can help."

"We're wolves," Oliver pointed out. "They'll be scared of us."

"I'll go on my own," Jessica offered. "Maybe they'll let me help." The other wolves looked to Oliver, who nodded once.

Jessica stood to her full height and walked slowly around the hedge and towards the reindeer. "Oh dear," the guarding reindeer said. "Please, wolf, we've had a difficult day. Just go and find something else to chase."

"You can talk?" Jessica said with surprise.

"Ah, not a wolf then, but a werewolf," the reindeer remarked. "My apologies."

"Yes," Jessica said. "We're all werewolves, and we want to help." As Jessica spoke, Oliver led the other wolves from behind the hedge and into the clearing.

"Thank you," the reindeer replied. "I'm Comet, and these are my brothers and sisters."

"Comet?" Kiera asked, rushing forwards. "Are your brothers and sisters Dasher, Dancer, Prancer, Vixen, Cupid, Donner, Blitzen and Rudolph?"

"Of course," Comet replied. "I thought the sleigh might have given it away."

"You're Father Christmas' reindeer," Hannah said with awe.

"What happened?" Jessica asked. "It isn't Christmas eve."

"Nick always likes to do a trial run a few nights before the main event," Comet informed them.

"Nick?" Oliver asked.

"Father Christmas. Santa Claus. Saint Nicholas. Pere

Noel. He has so many names across the world, it's easier just to call him Nick," Comet replied.

"So where is he?" Jessica persisted. "What happened?"

"We were flying low over the trees," Comet said, "when there was a loud bang beneath the sleigh. Moments after we crashed, two men arrived and dragged Nick away.

"I wanted to give chase, but so many of my brothers and sisters are injured I couldn't risk leaving them."

"Right then," Oliver said, stepping forwards. "Let's go and rescue Father Christmas!"

Chapter 4

"Thank you," Comet said, bowing slightly. "We've been so worried. Do you really think you can find him?"

"Which way did they take him?" Jessica asked.

"That way," Comet told her, pointing his hoof towards a cluster of trees. Jessica and the other wolves looked in the direction Comet was pointing. The snow was disturbed, marking a clear path that the wolves could follow.

"Do you have anything with his scent?" Oliver asked. "Just in case."

Comet thought about it for a moment before saying, "Check the sleigh. He's the only person who sits in there."

The wolves were beside themselves. To be able to actually get a look in Father Christmas' sleigh! It was like a dream come true.

13

Oliver went first and inspected the sleigh. The left runner was snapped in two and the right was twisted. Inside the sleigh, a plastic container holding two half-eaten sandwiches was lying on the floor. Oliver noticed the large box at the back of the sleigh was empty, before realising that it would only be full on Christmas Eve.

Father Christmas had a distinctive smell, and Oliver was able to fill his nostrils with it before allowing the other wolves to do the same. "He smells like cinnamon," Oliver mumbled to himself.

"He smells like chocolate orange," Jessica contradicted.

"I think he smells like cherries," Kiera added.

"No, it's eggnog, like the drink my dad always buys in Starbucks," Hannah said.

"Definitely gingerbread biscuits," William said.

"Wow," Oliver said at last. "He must smell like our favourite Christmas smells."

"Wow," the other wolves said wistfully as they enjoyed the Christmas memories the smells invoked.

"Ahem," Comet said. "Father Christmas?"

"Oh, yes," Oliver said sheepishly. "You're right. Come on, let's go!"

Oliver led the way. The men who had taken Father Christmas had done nothing to try to conceal their tracks, and following them was easy. The route took them through a cluster of trees and over a small hill, ending at a wooden shed.

"They must be in there," Oliver whispered. "Let's go and look."

Chapter 5

The wooden shed was small and had clearly seen better days. The single window had a pane of cracked class, and one wall was bowed, allowing the snow in at the corner.

"I'll go and look," William offered. "With my white fur, they won't see me in the snow."

"Okay," Oliver agreed. "Just be careful, we'll watch from here."

William crept slowly through the snow, wary of every sound and smell. The scent of gingerbread seemed to be everywhere, and definitely stronger the closer he got to the shed. As he thought about the sweet taste of gingerbread biscuits, his stomach rumbled loudly and he stopped instantly, making sure that the men inside hadn't heard.

After a minute, when it was clear that the men inside the shed hadn't heard, William continued, creeping even more slowly to the window. Cautiously, he raised himself up on his back legs and looked inside. The image filled him with horror, and he turned and ran as fast as he could back to the others.

"What is it?" Jessica asked as he arrived. "What did you see?"

"It's horrible," William said. "They've tied Father Christmas up, he's sat in a chair and he's got tape over his mouth. He looked really scared."

"Did you see the men?" Oliver asked.

"Yeah," William replied. "Two of them, just like Comet said. They looked mean."

"Who'd want to kidnap Father Christmas?" Kiera asked.

"Not everyone makes the nice list," Hannah replied.

"Maybe they want to steal his presents," Jessica suggested.

"He hasn't got any presents with him," Oliver reminded them.

"It doesn't matter why," William said. "He looked scared, we have to help him."

"William's right," Jessica agreed. "It doesn't matter why they kidnapped him, we have to rescue him."

"So what do we do?" Oliver asked.

"Easy," Jessica said, before beginning to describe her plan.

Chapter 6

Jessica went to the shed door while the other wolves hid. Jessica scraped her paw against the door and whimpered pathetically.

"What's that noise?" one of the men said gruffly.

"I don't know, do I?" the other man said. "Why don't you go and look?"

"Why don't you go and look?" the first man said.

"Cause I told you to look, didn't I!" the second man said angrily.

"You aint the boss of me!" the first man said.

"Mum said different," the second man said.

"When?" the first man asked, clearly upset.

"When you was upstairs," the second man announced.

"She said I'm the boss, and you got to do as I say."

"Really?" the first man asked. His voice was quivering, as though he was about to cry. "Mum said that?"

"Yeah, so go and see what that noise was," the second man said triumphantly.

The first man opened the door and saw a weary looking wolf sat in the snow at his feet. The wolf whimpered, as though in pain, and began to hobble away as the man looked down at her.

"It's a dog," the first man said. "Looks hurt."

"Just shut the door then," the second man said. "You're letting the cold in."

"Come here little doggie," the first man said. "I won't hurt you."

"Little doggie?" the second man said, joining his brother at the door. "It's nearly as big as you."

Jessica whimpered again and crept further away from the two men before collapsing in the snow, pretending to be unable to move any further.

"Let's bring it inside," the first man said. "It's hurt. Do you think mum will let us keep it?"

"Not after what happened to your hamster," the second man said. "She still has nightmares."

"That was an accident," the first man said. "Come on, help me bring it inside."

The second man gruffed and grumbled before joining his brother in attempting to pick Jessica up. Just as they slipped their arms around her, the other wolves ran from the back of the shed and began to bark and growl loudly behind the two men.

"What's going on?" both men exclaimed, dropping Jessica in the process. Jessica landed on her feet and began to bark and growl just as loudly as the other wolves.

"I thought you said it was hurt?" the second man said, backing away from Jessica and the other wolves.

"I thought it was," the first man said.

The five wolves were slowly driving the two men away from the shed, barking and growling and being as fierce and menacing as possible. "Now!" Oliver said, though to the two men it sounded like a particularly aggressive snarl.

The wolves got louder and louder, barking for all they were worth. The two men began to cower and hold each other. William suddenly sprinted forwards and sunk his sharp teeth into the first man's leg, making the man cry out in pain.

"That's it," the first man screamed. "Let's get out of here."

"What about Father Christmas?" the second man asked nervously, but the first man was already running as fast as he could towards the edge of Swanholme Park. Within seconds, the second man was sprinting after him.

"Well done, Jessica," Oliver said. "That worked brilliantly."

"Thanks," Jessica replied. "Let's go and untie Father Christmas!"

Chapter 7

The werewolves made short work of Father's Christmas' bonds, chewing through the ropes and pulling the tape from his mouth. Father Christmas stood slowly and listened to his joints creak as he worked away the tension in his arms and legs.

"Thank you, children," he said, his voice deep and booming. "However did you find me?"

"It was Comet," Jessica replied. "He showed us which way the men took you."

"Ho ho ho," Father Christmas laughed. "He really saved my bacon! I'll be sure to give him an extra carrot when we get back to the North Pole."

"Are you okay?" Oliver asked. "Did those men hurt you?"

"Thomas and Justin," Father Christmas muttered to himself. "They've been on the naughty list for as long as I can remember. No, they didn't hurt me, but they won't be getting any presents, that's for sure!"

"What did they want?" William asked.

"That is interesting," Father Christmas replied. "They didn't want anything, at least as far as I could tell. Apparently, their mother told them to hold me until Boxing Day, and then they could let me go."

"Why Boxing Day?" William prompted.

"I'm not sure," Father Christmas said. "But Christmas would have been ruined if you hadn't rescued me."

That made all the wolves smile. "Do you know who their mother is?" Oliver asked, remembering that the Witch who had poisoned the school meals had been hired by a woman.

"I remember her as a little girl," Father Christmas mused. "Marjorie, on the nice list as I recall. I don't know why she'd do this."

"Marjorie?" Jessica said out loud. "Do we know anyone called Marjorie?" The other wolves thought hard about it, thinking of their parents names and any other adults that they knew.

"Do you know her surname?" Kiera asked.

"Ho ho ho," Father Christmas laughed. "Surnames are for your parents and teachers, I only need your first name to know if you've been naughty or nice."

The werewolves thought about it some more. "I don't think I know anyone called Marjorie," Oliver admitted at last."

"Me either," Jessica agreed. The other wolves shook their head in unison.

"Then if you would be so kind," Father Christmas asked, "perhaps you could show me back to my sleigh?"

Chapter 8

Oliver led the way, over the small hill and through the cluster of trees and back to the sleigh. "Nick!" Comet said excitedly as he ran towards Father Christmas.

"I hear I have you to thank for my rescue?" Father Christmas said.

"We were just lucky these young werewolves came along when they did," Comet replied.

"That we were," Father Christmas agreed. "Now, I think our test flight is over. How do you feel about returning to the North Pole?"

"Ah," Comet said sheepishly. "I think we might have a problem."

Father Christmas turned and looked at the other reindeer and the broken sleigh. "Oh dear," he said, shaking his head.

"Rudolph and Blitzen should be able to fly," Comet continued, "but my other brothers and sisters are far too injured."

"Oh no, Father Christmas," Jessica said nervously. "Can't you heal them?"

"I can," Father Christmas said, "but sadly not here. The magic I need for healing them is only found at the North Pole."

"Can we help?" Hannah asked. "We'll do anything, really."

"Ho ho ho," Father Christmas laughed. "You are good girls and boys. Let's see now, hmm."

Father Christmas walked over to the sleigh and pulled it from the snow. The damaged runners creaked and groaned as he did so. "This won't do," he said to himself. "This won't do at all."

Father Christmas turned the sleigh upside down and began to bend and shape the runners with his bare hands. As he worked, he whistled Jingle Bells to himself.

"Comet," he said. "Please fetch me my tools."

Comet smiled and slid his head under the upturned sleigh, returning with a shiny red tool box hanging from his mouth. Father Christmas ruffled the fur on Comet's head before retrieving a strange looking screwdriver from the box.

"Cover your eyes, children," Father Christmas said, prompting the wolves to place their paws over their eyes. Comet turned away too as Father Christmas placed the tip of the screwdriver against the runners. Blue sparks lit up the night sky and suddenly both runners looked to be back to normal.

"Wow," Oliver said. "That's amazing."

"Magic screwdriver," Father Christmas said with a wink. "Now, how would you wolves feel about pulling my sleigh?"

Chapter 9

"What, really?" William asked excitedly. "Like pull the sleigh, for real?"

"Ho ho ho," Father Christmas laughed. "I'll take that as a yes?"

"Yes!" William replied, panting a little as his tongue lolled from his mouth and his tail wagged furiously.

"Rudolph, you'll be at the front as usual," Father Christmas continued. "And Comet and Blitzen, you'll be next. Then the wolves will help give us a little extra oomph!"

"Perfect," Comet replied. "I'll help the others into the sleigh."

Father Christmas turned the sleigh over and Comet helped the wounded reindeer aboard. "It's going to be a tight fit," Comet said.

"We'll manage," Father Christmas replied. "Now, children, if you would kindly line up in front of the sleigh."

Jessica and the other wolves lined up as requested, Jessica and Oliver to one side in one line, and William, Kiera and Hannah in another. Father Christmas attached a collar to each of them before securing it to the sleigh with a fine golden thread.

"How does that feel?" Father Christmas asked. "Not too tight, I hope?"

"It's fine," Jessica replied. "Nice and warm, actually."

"How are we going to get all the way to the North Pole?" William asked. "It's miles away."

"Ho ho ho," Father Christmas laughed. "How do you think? We'll fly of course!"

Without another word, Father Christmas began to rub his hands together and mutter secret words under his breath. As the wolves watched, faint blue sparks seemed to drift from his fingertips, dancing across the werewolves fur.

Jessica and the others began to feel their bodies tingle, similar to when they changed on the night of the full moon. It was like being tickled with a feather, but as soon as it started it was gone.

"There we are," Father Christmas said, smiling to

himself. "That should be plenty to get us back to the North Pole. Rudolph, are we ready?"

"Ready when you are, Nick," Rudolph said, his nose beginning to glow. "Just say the word."

Father Christmas climbed into the sleigh and made himself comfortable before shouting, "Lentaa!"

Chapter 10

Rudolph began to run, slowly at first but quickly building up speed. Comet and Blitzen joined in, followed by the werewolves. The sleigh seemed heavy at first, but soon it was sliding along behind them. With one almighty jump, Rudolph leapt into the air and kept on climbing.

Jessica and the other wolves suddenly found their paws no longer touching the ground as they were drawn into the air. "We're flying!" William squealed.

"This is incredible," Jessica replied.

"Awesome!" Oliver added.

The sleigh rose higher and higher, reindeer and wolf legs running as fast as they could. Once through the clouds, Rudolph turned towards the North Star and led them all the way to the North Pole.

The flight seemed to take hours, but the reindeer and

wolves never felt tired, and the moon never moved in the sky. They passed over towns and cities, rolling fields and deep oceans. Oliver spotted the fjords of Norway and the forests of Finland, before all he could see below him was the white ice and snow of the Arctic.

After countless hours, Rudolph began to descend, guiding the sleigh back towards the ground. A faint light in the distance seemed to guide them, slowly growing brighter as they neared. "Prepare to touch down," Rudolph called, and a moment later their legs were pounding against the snow and they pulled the sleigh towards the light.

"Pysakki!" Father Christmas called (which sounded like fu-sa-ki), and Rudolph and the other reindeer began to slow down. Rudolph steered the sleigh to the right of the light and the wolves suddenly found themselves inside a large stable, though they didn't remember seeing a door.

"Ho ho ho," Father Christmas laughed as he stepped down from the sleigh. "Well done, all of you."

"Thank you," Jessica said. "Where are we?"

"At the North Pole, of course," Father Christmas replied.

"No, I mean, here?" Jessica continued. "How did we get in here?"

"Ah," Father Christmas said. "With all those pesky

satellites and Arctic explorers, I've had to hide my home and factory. From the outside, it looks just like all the other snow and ice. Only me and my Reindeer know how to find the secret door."

"Brilliant!" William said.

"What about our mums and dads?" Oliver asked nervously. "We've been gone for hours, they'll be looking for us."

"Ho ho ho," Father Christmas laughed again. "No time has passed at all since we left. How else would I be able to deliver presents to all the boys and girls in a single night? Time won't start again until you're safely back in Swanholme Park."

"Brilliant!" William said again.

"Now, lets see about healing the rest of my reindeer," Father Christmas said.

After releasing the wolves from their collars, Father Christmas helped the injured reindeer from the sleigh and into the stalls. Once inside, he poured each of them a drink from a shiny green flask and, after drinking it, each of the reindeer looked to be back to normal.

"Wow," Jessica asked once Father Christmas had finished. "What was in that drink?"

"Just a little magic," Father Christmas replied with a wink. "Now, how about I show you around?"

Chapter 11

Jessica and the others couldn't believe their ears. They were actually going to get to look at where Father Christmas made his toys. No one would ever believe them.

After making sure that the reindeer had plenty of food and water, Father Christmas led the wolves from the stables and into a large kitchen where a roaring fire burned in the stove. Stood at the stove was an elderly woman, dressed in red just like Father Christmas.

"You're late, Nick," she said with a twinkle in her eye. "And I see you've brought guests."

"Mary," Father Christmas replied. "These clever young werewolves really saved my bacon. I'll tell you all about it after I given them the grand tour!"

"I'll make sure there's extra hot chocolate for when you've finished," Mary replied.

Father Christmas took a moment to kiss Mary on the cheek before leading the wolves into the next room. It was like nothing they had ever imagined. The room was huge, bigger than any they had ever seen, with millions of tables and ladders that led up and down to a multitude of levels.

At each table, an elf was busy hammering or fixing toys together, whistling a variety of Christmas tunes as they enjoyed their work. "This is my factory," Father Christmas said with pride. "Here, my elves and I make all the toys."

"All the toys?" Hannah asked, a little bewildered by the size of the factory.

"My elves work all year long just to make sure the toys are ready in time," Father Christmas added.

Father Christmas led them from the factory to a beautiful walled garden, full of trees and flowers. Overhead, the sky was full of stars, and outside the snow was still falling, but it didn't seen to effect the plants at all.

"This is beautiful," Kiera said.

"It is, isn't it," Father Christmas said with a smile. "Mary and I always enjoy our time here on Christmas morning, exchanging gifts."

"You get Christmas presents too?" Oliver asked.

"Of course!" Father Christmas replied. "I'm always on the nice list."

That made the werewolves laugh out loud, and Father Christmas let them run and jump and play in his magical secret garden while Mary finished warming the hot chocolate.

#

Some time later, Father Christmas called the wolves back to the kitchen where five bowls of steaming hot chocolate waited for them. Mary had lined them up on the floor, and the wolves lapped it up hungrily.

"This is the best hot chocolate I've ever had," Jessica said.

"It really is," Oliver agreed.

"I can't believe we have to go home soon," William grumbled.

"If you don't go home, it will never be Christmas," Father Christmas reminded them.

"Oh, yeah," William remembered. "Am I getting a new Playstation?"

"Ho ho ho," Father Christmas laughed. "That depends on whether you're on my nice list or not."

"Ah, erm," William stuttered, making everyone else laugh out loud.

"I think you'll all be getting a nice surprise Christmas morning," Father Christmas said with a wink.

After finishing their hot chocolate, Father Christmas led them back to the stables, where Rudolph was waiting for them. "I'll show you the way home," Rudolph said, his red nose beginning to glow.

"How do we get back?" Kiera asked.

"The flight magic will last until you return to Swanholme Park," Father Christmas said.

"Are you coming too?" Jessica asked.

"Sadly not," Father Christmas replied. "I really have to make sure everything is ready for Christmas eve."

"Thank you, Father Christmas," Jessica said sincerely.

"No, thank you, children," Father Christmas replied. "And make sure to be asleep early on Christmas Eve, it's true I can't bring your presents unless you're asleep."

"This way," Rudolph said as he began a slow trot from the stables. He gradually got faster and faster, and the wolves had to work hard to keep up. Suddenly, there was snow and ice beneath their paws, and with an almighty leap, Rudolph leapt into the air and continued climbing.

"Brilliant!" William shouted as the wolves began to ascend with him.

"Come quickly," Jessica's dad shouted from the bottom of the stairs. "He's been!"

Jessica darted from her room and straight down the stairs, almost knocking her dad over in the process. "Did he bring me something?" Jessica asked hurriedly.

"I think you'll be pleasantly surprised," Jessica's dad remarked.

Jessica stepped into the living room to find a small mountain of presents surrounding the Christmas tree. "Are they all for me?" she asked.

"The labels say so," Jessica's mum replied. "Which one do you want to open first?"

Jessica was overwhelmed. There were presents of all shapes and sizes and she didn't know where to begin. In the end, she pulled the package from the top and tore the paper open.

"From Comet," Jessica said to herself as she read the label.

"Comet?" Jessica's dad asked.

"He's one of Father Christmas' reindeer," Jessica replied. As she opened the box, she found a furry collar inside, just like the one she had worn when pulling the sleigh.

"Why would Father Christmas give you a dog collar?" Jessica's dad asked with surprise. "Is there a note?"

Jessica looked under the collar and found a small handwritten note. *Just in case we need you next year*, it said.

"I can't tell you, dad," Jessica said with a smile. "It's a secret."

Father Christmas' words

Father Christmas used two words when commanding the reindeer (and the werewolves) to pull the sleigh. The words I chose are from Finland, where reindeer come from.

Lentaa means fly.

Psyakki means stop.

They aren't the real words Father Christmas uses, I asked him. Have you any idea how much it costs to call the North Pole? Well I do, and it's a lot! And do you know what he said? They're secret. The magic words he uses to make his reindeer fly are secret.

Hmmph.

Books by R. Jackson-Lawrence

<u>PUPS</u>
The Case of the Horrifying Headmaster
The Case of the Loathsome Lunches
The case of the Cancelled Christmas
The Case of the Mischievous Mummy
The Case of the Atrocious Amulet
The Case of the Egg-cellent Easter
The Case of the Ghastly Ghost
The Case of the Terrible Truth

<u>The Chronicle of Benjamin Knight</u>
Knightfall
Darkest Before Dawn
New Light

Made in the USA
Middletown, DE
15 May 2016